First published 1989 by Julia MacRae Books
Published 1992 by Walker Books Ltd
87 Vauxhall Walk, London SE11 5HJ

16 18 20 19 17 15

© 1989 Anthony Browne

The right of Anthony Browne to be identified as author/illustrator of this work has been asserted
by him accordance with the Copyright, Designs and Patents Act 1988

This book has been set in Futura Light

Printed in China

British Library Cataloguing in Publication Data:
a catalogue record for this book is available from the British Library

ISBN 978-1-4063-1329-1

www.walker.co.uk

The Tunnel

Anthony Browne

WALKER BOOKS
AND SUBSIDIARIES
LONDON • BOSTON • SYDNEY • AUCKLAND

Once upon a time there lived a sister and brother who were not at all alike. In every way they were different.

The sister stayed inside on her own, reading and dreaming.
The brother played outside with his friends, laughing and
shouting, throwing and kicking, roughing and tumbling.

At night he slept soundly in his room. But she would lie awake, listening to the noises of the night. Sometimes he crept into her room to frighten her, for he knew that she was afraid of the dark.

Whenever they were together they fought and argued noisily. All the time.

One morning their mother grew impatient with them.
"Out you go together," she said, "and try to be nice to each
other just for once. And be back in time for lunch." But the
boy didn't want his little sister with him.

They went to a piece of waste ground.

"Why did you have to come?" he moaned.

"It's not my fault," she said. "I didn't want to come
to this awful place. It scares me."

"Oh, you baby," said her brother. "You're frightened
of everything." He went off to explore.

His sister was frightened of the tunnel and so she waited for him to come out again. She waited and waited, but he did not come. She was close to tears. What could she do? She had to follow him into the tunnel.

The tunnel was dark,

and damp, and slimy, and scary.

At the other end she found herself in a quiet wood. There was no sign of her brother. But the wood soon turned into a dark forest. She thought about wolves and giants and witches, and wanted to turn back, but she could not – for what would become of her brother if she did? By now she was very frightened and she began to run, faster and faster…

Just when she knew she could run no further,
she came to a clearing.
There was a figure, still as stone.
It was her brother.
"Oh no!" she sobbed. "I'm too late."

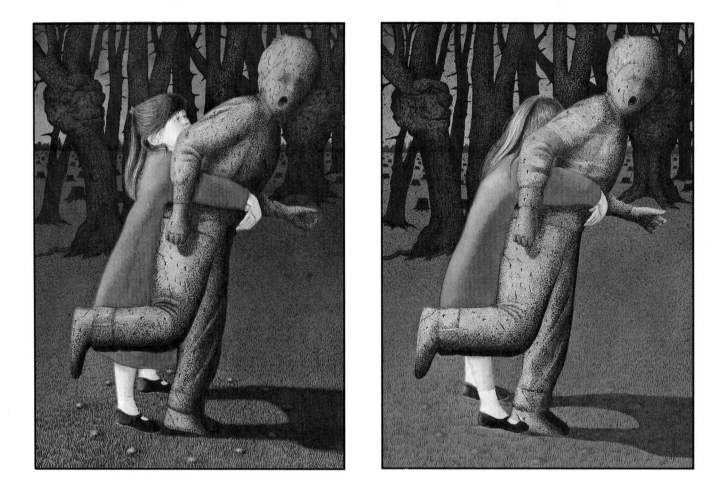

She threw her arms around the cold hard form, and wept.
Very slowly, the figure began to change colour, becoming
softer and warmer.

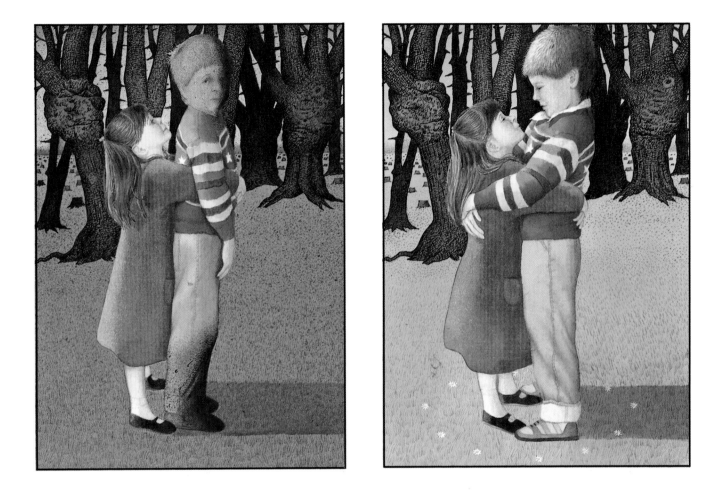

Then, little by little, it began to move. Her brother was there. "Rose! I knew you'd come," he said. They ran back, through the forest, through the wood, into the tunnel, and out again. **Together.**

When they reached home, their mother was setting the table.

"Hello," she said, "you two seem very quiet.

Is everything all right?"

Rose smiled at her brother.

And Jack smiled back.

Anthony Browne

Winner of multiple awards including the prestigious Kate Greenaway Medal and the much-coveted Hans Christian Andersen Award, Anthony is one of the most celebrated author–illustrators of his generation. Renowned for his unique style his work is recognized and loved throughout the world.

ISBN 978-1-4063-1930-9

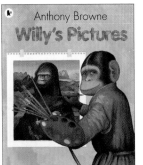

ISBN 978-1-4063-1356-7

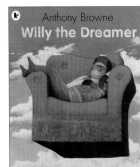

ISBN 978-1-4063-1357-4

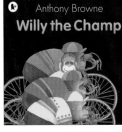

ISBN 978-1-4063-1873-9

ISBN 978-1-4063-1327-7

ISBN 978-1-4063-1329-1

ISBN 978-0-7445-9858-2

ISBN 978-0-7445-9857-5

ISBN 978-1-4063-1852-4

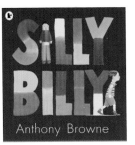

ISBN 978-1-4063-0576-0

ISBN 978-1-4063-1328-4

ISBN 978-1-4063-1339-0

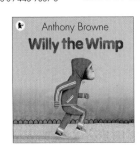

ISBN 978-1-4063-1874-6

Available from all good bookstores

www.walker.co.uk